Flor's Journey to Independence

Flor's Journey to Independence

Barbara Vaille and
Jennifer QuinnWilliams

Illustrations by Barbara Goodsitt

THE UNIVERSITY OF MICHIGAN PRESS
Ann Arbor

ISBN 0-472-03107-4
Published in the United States of America
The University of Michigan Press
Manufactured in the United States of America
⊗ Printed on acid-free paper

2008 2007 2006 2005 4 3 2 1

To the Reader:

This book was written for your pleasure. It is written in simple English for adult language learners. We hope you will enjoy the story and learn English at the same time. Note that when a character is speaking in Spanish, the speech appears in *italics* (even though it will appear in English). When a character is speaking in English, the type does not change.

Happy Reading,
Barbara and Jennifer
Denver, CO

BUS
DENVER

CHAPTER 1

Flor Pacheco stood up from her bus seat and stepped into the aisle. She reached above her head for the suitcase on the rack over the seat. They were home. Flor and Betina, her four-year-old daughter, were back in Denver after three months in Mexico visiting her parents. Those three months passed by so quickly. Flor gently patted Betina on the back.

"Wake up, Little One."

Betina slowly raised her head.

"Mama, where are we?" asked Betina. She rubbed her eyes and stood up on the bus seat. *"Are we here?"*

Flor smiled at her little daughter and pushed her thick black hair away from her face.

"Yes, we are here! Look out the window and see if your father is waiting."

"I see lots of people!"

"OK. Let's go."

Flor and Betina climbed down the bus stairs. They stood there in the bright light of the afternoon and looked at the crowd of happy relatives meeting fathers, brothers, cousins, and mothers. She did not see her own husband, Ricardo. Was he late?

She found her three suitcases in the pile by the bus and moved them, one by one, to the side of the small bus station. Betina followed.

"Mama, I am thirsty," she said.

"You can have a drink when we get home."

"I am thirsty now."

Where was Ricardo? Betina was very tired and would soon begin to cry. The sun was hot on Flor's face, and the bus station was dusty. People got into cars and left. Soon, she and Betina would be alone. She didn't want to leave the suitcases to go get Betina a drink, and she didn't want to carry them into the station and back out again.

"When we get home, Little One, when we get home," she said.

"Let's go home now!"

Flor wiped her face with her hand. It was hot in the sun. She did not remember Denver being so hot. She looked at her watch. Ricardo was already an hour late. Maybe he didn't know what time the bus arrived. The last time she talked to him was many weeks ago. After that, he was never home when she called on the telephone.

Betina began to cry. *"Where is Daddy? I want to go home."*

Flor picked up Betina and held her. She looked through the dirty window into the bus station and noticed that there were pop machines next to the telephone. She made a decision.

"OK, let's go," she said. She left the suitcases

and went into the station. She bought Betina a Sprite® and walked over to the telephone. A card on the wall by the phone said, "TAXI! *Se habla español.* (We speak Spanish.)" Flor called the number and ordered a taxi. It would be expensive, but she and Betina must get home somehow.

The taxi driver was very nice. He helped Flor carry the suitcases up to her apartment door. She gave him a two-dollar tip. Ricardo would say it was too much, but Ricardo wasn't there to help her, was he?

Flor turned the key in the lock of the door and gave it a push. It opened and revealed a large, sunny room with no furniture. The apartment was empty. Flor gasped and pulled the door shut again. This was not her apartment. The apartment she lived in had nice chairs and tables, and curtains on the windows. She looked at the number: 301. That was her apartment number. Of course, her key wouldn't open another door, only her own.

She opened the door again and walked in slowly. Betina held Flor's hand tightly.

"Mama, we're not home. This is not where we live. I want to go back to Grandma and Grandpa's house."

Flor did not answer Betina. What had happened? Where were the sofa and the big chair? Where was the television? Where were the kitchen table and the four chairs that she and Ricardo bought at Target™ just six months ago? There were no pictures on the wall, and no telephone in the kitchen. She opened the refrigerator. Empty. She opened the cupboards. Empty. She looked in the bedrooms. Empty.

Betina began to cry again.

"Where is Papa? I want to go back to Grandma and Grandpa's house!"

Flor shook Betina's little arm. *"Be quiet!"* she said.

Betina cried more loudly. *"Ow! You hurt me! I want my papa! I want my grandma!"*

Suddenly, Flor wanted to cry, too. Why had she left Mexico? Ricardo was missing and so was almost everything she owned in the world. Did someone kill Ricardo and rob the apartment? Was that the reason he didn't meet the bus? She knelt down on the floor and hugged her little girl, her little love, to her chest.

"OK, OK, Betina-tina," she said. *"OK, OK. Mama will make it better."*

Betina cuddled up to Flor, who picked her up and walked down the stairs to the manager's apartment. She had a telephone. *"We will tell Aunt Maria,"* she said to Betina as they walked. *"When she and Papa moved to America with your grandma they learned English in school. Aunt Maria will call the police and tell them that we were robbed. She will help us find Papa."*

The apartment manager was a friendly, older American woman who spoke only two words of

Spanish. She could say, *"Hola"* and *"Adios."* When she saw Flor, she looked surprised.

"Hola," she said.

"Hola," said Flor. "Telephone, please?"

"Sure, sure," said the apartment manager. She kept talking as she led Flor and Betina to the telephone, but Flor only understood a few words. Ricardo spoke English, and he always told Flor she didn't need to speak it. Flor smiled and nodded her head, and the manager held out her hand to Betina.

"Do you want a cookie?"

Flor and Betina understood "cookie," and they both nodded.

"Thank you, thank you," said Flor.

"Thank you," said Betina. The manager led Betina into the kitchen, still saying things in the English that Flor could not understand.

Maria answered the telephone on the first ring.

"Hola," she said.

Flor felt so happy to hear Maria's voice and to hear someone speaking Spanish. *"Maria, we were robbed! Everything is gone! The apartment is empty, and Ricardo never came to the bus to meet us! I'm so worried. I'm so frightened."*

"Flor?"

"Yes, of course I'm Flor. We were robbed! Do you know where Ricardo is?"

"Calm down, Flor." Maria sounded strange. Not friendly. *"Where are you? How do you know the apartment is empty?"*

Flor thought this was an odd question. *"We're here in Denver, at the apartment."*

"What are you doing here?"

"This is September! Don't you remember? I said I would come back to Denver in September."

"Ricardo told you not to come." Now Maria sounded angry.

"But Maria, you do not understand. . . ."

Maria interrupted her. *"No, Flor, you do not understand. Ricardo called you in Mexico and told you not to come back to Denver. He called you last week. He said you were surprised and angry, but I didn't think you would be this foolish! Why did you return?"*

"I didn't talk to Ricardo. Why did he want me to stay in Mexico?"

"There is no place for you and Betina in his life. He wanted you to stay with your mother and father."

Flor was so confused she could barely speak. Was she going crazy?

"What are you saying? I am Ricardo's wife. Betina is Ricardo's daughter. Where is he? I want to talk to him about this."

"No. It is final. Ricardo lives with his new family now," said Maria.

Flor felt dizzy. She stared at the phone in her hand. When she finally put it to her ear again, Maria was shouting, *"Flor, Flor, are you there?"*

She sounded worried, a little more like the Maria that Flor knew. Maria was Betina's godmother. Flor and Ricardo stayed with Maria and Ricardo's mother when they first lived together. Flor thought Maria was her good friend.

"Sorry. Sorry, Maria. You said . . . you said. . . ."

"New family."

"Oh, my."

"You were gone a long time, Flor. Ricardo got lonely."

"I was gone three months! That's not so long! Three months!"

Maria was silent. Flor felt sick. What was she going to do? They needed help from Maria. She breathed deeply and asked for help.

"I need several things. I need towels and blankets and cooking pots and beds. Ricardo must bring me these things. Give me his phone number."

Maria did not answer.

"Maria?"

"Tomorrow, Flor. Call me tomorrow."

Maria hung up the telephone.

Flor stared at the phone in her hand. Tomorrow? They needed help today.

The manager returned from the kitchen with Betina, who was eating one cookie and holding another one.

"Bad news?" asked the manager.

Flor understood "bad," but she did not want the manager to know about her troubles.

She forced herself to smile.

"OK, thank you," she said. She took Betina's

hand and led her back to the empty apartment. She gave Betina her doll and went into the bathroom. She stared at her face in the mirror. Was this the same pretty, round face Ricardo kissed three months ago? What was she going to do? Ricardo and Betina were all she had in America. Now, she only had Betina.

CHAPTER 2

The rest of the afternoon passed. Flor felt strange. She felt like she was under water. She moved slowly, and she wasn't thinking clearly. When Betina got hungry, Flor cut up two apples she had in her bag. When it got dark, Flor found her bathrobe, two sweaters, and her winter coat still hanging in her closet. She made a bed with them on the floor for Betina and herself.

"*Come lie down, Little One. It's time for bed.*" Flor tucked Betina in with her jacket and lay down beside her. She closed her eyes but couldn't sleep. She wondered who paid the rent on the apartment while she was gone. Had someone been living here? Did Ricardo and his new family live here while she was in Mexico? When did they move out? Today? Just before she arrived on the bus? Or when she tried to call him from Mexico? She pictured Ricardo with another woman. Who was Ricardo's new wife? Where did he meet her? Did Flor know her? Questions, questions, questions, and no answers. Flor tossed and turned. Luckily, Betina was so tired from the journey that she slept through the night.

When morning came, Flor was worried and tired, and Betina was hungry. Flor folded up the clothes that had been the makeshift bed. Then she and Betina walked to the little store down the street to buy bread and milk. Flor looked at the pay phone on the corner. *"I should call Maria right now,"* she thought. Betina pulled on her arm.

"Mama, Mama. I'm hungry."

"OK, Little One. Let's go home."

Back at the apartment, Flor put bread and milk on the floor by the window for Betina.

"You can have a picnic with your doll," she said. *"I'll be right back. I have to go call Aunt Maria."*

"I want to come, too."

"No. You stay here and eat your breakfast. I'll be back in a minute."

"OK, Mama."

Flor hurried back to the pay phone and called her sister-in-law. *"Maria, this is Flor. Where is Ricardo? I must talk to him."*

"Hi, Flor. I-I-I don't know."

"Maria, it's important. I need money. There's nothing in the apartment, no furniture, no food, nothing! What am I supposed to do? And what about Betina? She's his daughter! Doesn't he want to see her?"

"Calm down, Flor. I'll talk to Ricardo. This afternoon, I'll bring you the things you asked for—some

dishes and towels and blankets. I'll come about 1:00, OK?"

"OK. Thanks, Maria. We'll be at home." Flor hung up the phone. It was only 8:30. What would she and Betina do until Maria came? She hurried home.

Betina was standing by the window, holding her doll. She looked a little scared.

"Betina, here I am. Did you have enough to eat? Do you want some more bread?"

"No. Where were you, Mama? You were gone a long time," she said in a quiet voice.

"I was at the pay phone talking to Aunt Maria. I tried to hurry. I'm sorry it seemed like such a long time. Hey, what shall we do today? Maria is coming over after lunch. Let's go somewhere fun this morning. Do you want to go to the zoo?"

"Oh, yes! Can we go now?"

Flor laughed. She was so glad she had Betina. What a joy she was!

"Yes, let's go. There's nothing to do here. Let me think. We can walk to the school—that's two blocks away—and catch the number 10 bus there. That will take us right to the zoo. We'll be there when it opens. How does that sound?"

"Fun! Can I take my doll?"

"Sure. You hold her hand, and I'll hold yours."

They walked down the street toward the bus stop, past old houses and big square apartment buildings. Some had peeling paint and litter; others had lush green grass and pretty flowers. They passed a bagel shop, a hardware store, and a dry cleaner. They stopped at a red light in front of a Burger King®. A sign in the window caught Flor's eye—NOW HIRING. *"Maybe I can get a job here,"* she thought. *"It's close to home. But if I need to know English, that's a problem. I'll come back this afternoon when Maria comes over. I'll ask her to watch Betina."*

The light changed. They crossed the street and walked down to the bus stop by the school.

"Where's the bus, Mama?" Betina asked.

"It will be here in a few minutes. Look at the apple and leaf decorations in the school windows. School started last week."

"I want to go to school. Can I go to school?"

"Next year you can start kindergarten. You have to be five years old. Here comes the bus."

They got on the bus, paid the fare, and sat near the front.

"My dolly likes to ride the bus, Mama. She likes to look out the window and see the pretty trees and houses."

"That's nice, Little One," Flor said. Her mind was a million miles away. If she closed her eyes, she saw Ricardo, so she kept them open. Luckily, Betina was happy now and didn't notice how quiet her mother was.

"The zoo," the bus driver said, announcing the stop.

"Here we are, Betina. Do you have your doll?"

"Yes," she answered. They got off the bus. It was a beautiful fall day. The sky was blue. The sun was shining. Flor and Betina walked slowly by the camels and buffaloes, past the giraffes and elephants, and over to the monkeys. Betina was excited by everything. Flor hardly saw anything; she was so worried. Ricardo. Money. Food. Betina. Baby-sitter. Burger King. English. . . .

"I'm hungry, Mama."

"So am I. Let's get a hot dog at the cart in front of the zoo. It's time to catch the bus so we are home when Aunt Maria comes."

Maria's hands were full when she arrived. She had the dishes and linens plus a sack of groceries and a frying pan. She didn't look happy.

"Oh, Maria, let me take something. Come in!"

"Here. I can't stay long."

Flor felt like crying. Maria didn't even say hello. She didn't say "welcome back" or even hug Betina. She didn't seem friendly.

"I'm sorry, Maria," she said. *"But I need a little more help. Can you stay with Betina for a few minutes? I want to go see about a job."*

"A job? Where?" asked Maria.

"I can't tell you yet. Please? I'll be back as soon as I can. It's not far away," answered Flor.

"Well. . . . OK. . . . but I have to be home soon. Hurry!"

Flor raced out the door calling, *"I will. Thanks. Bye."*

Suddenly, at the door to Burger King, Flor was scared. Even after living in America for five years, she knew almost no English. It was not too difficult to get around without it. At the clinic and most stores, someone spoke Spanish. She listened to the Spanish stations on the radio and watched the Spanish channels on TV. Their friends were all from Mexico, and Ricardo spoke English. Ricardo. The thought of him made her push the door open.

Only a few people were sitting at tables eating. No one was in line. Flor went up to the counter. A friendly looking man in his thirties said, "Can I take your order?"

"No. Now hiring?" Flor asked in English, pointing to herself.

"Oh. Do you speak Spanish?" the man asked her in Spanish.

"Yes!" Flor answered. *"I came about the job here. I saw the sign in your window."*

"I'm the manager. Here's an application. You can fill it out now."

He handed her the form. She paused. The manager said, *"It's in English, so if you have any questions, just ask. I'll be behind the counter. My name is David."*

"Nice to meet you. My name is Flor." She took

BURGER KING

the application, sat down at an open table, and looked at it. Name. Address. Social Security Number—luckily, she had one. Good thing she had filed for it last year. Phone—no phone! She filled it out and only had a question about the Work Experience section. She went to the counter and asked David, *"What does this mean?"*

"It means, what jobs have you had before?"

"Oh. I have never worked. I stay home with my little girl, and my hus—I mean my-uh-" she stammered.

"That's OK. We train our employees here. This application looks fine. We need someone right away to work in the back as a short-order cook, cooking the burgers and fries and making salads. The pay is $6.50 an hour. It's for the 11:00 AM to 7:00 PM shift, Monday through Friday. Linda, the assistant manager will be in at 6:00 tonight. Can you come back then? She can show you what you need to do. She speaks Spanish, too. You can start tomorrow then, alright?"

Flor wasn't sure if she understood him. Even though David's Spanish was good, he had an American accent. *"Do you mean I have the job?"*

"Yes." David smiled. *"Come at 6:00. I work until 7:00 tonight, so I'll still be here when you come. See you then."*

Flor looked at him and smiled back. *"OK. Thank you."* Flor left the restaurant, still smiling, and hurried home. Suddenly she stopped. *"Oh no!"*

she thought. *"What have I done? What about Betina? Who will take care of her?"*

Maria and Betina were sitting on the floor playing with her doll when Flor returned.

"Hi, Mama. Aunt Maria and I are playing house with my dolly."

"That's nice, Little One. Maria, can you come in the other room for a minute? I have something to tell you."

The two women left Betina by herself. *"Maria, I got a job!"*

"What? Where? When?" Maria asked. She could not believe it.

"Right now! A minute ago. I saw a sign in the window at Burger King this morning when Betina and I went to the zoo. Just now I went in and filled out an application, and the manager said I have the job! I go back in tonight to train with the assistant manager. I'm so excited, but I didn't think about Betina. Will you do me a big, big favor and take her home? Let her spend the night with you. Please!" Flor begged.

"I don't know. I was thinking of going out. . . ."

"Please, Maria! I'll return the favor. I swear I will," pleaded Flor.

"OK, just this once. I love Betina, but I can't make up for what my brother did, and I'm not going to try," Maria said.

"I know. It's not your problem. But I don't know what else to do. Thanks, Maria."

Flor and Maria went back into the living room to tell Betina the plans.

"Guess what, Betina? Aunt Maria is taking you home to spend the night with her and Grandma. Won't that be fun?"

"Can I take my dolly?"

"Of course," said her mother. *"Let's put your sweater and a few other things in a bag for you. Aunt Maria needs to get home."* In a minute, they were ready to go.

"Bye, Little One. Have a good time. I'll see you tomorrow. Give Grandma a kiss for me." Flor gave Betina a hug and turned to Maria. *"Thanks again, Maria,"* and gave her a hug, too. Just as they turned to leave, Maria handed Flor a scrap of paper with a phone number on it.

"Ricardo," she said.

CHAPTER 3

At a little after 9:00 that night, Flor climbed the stairs to her apartment. Her head was full of phrases and instructions that Linda, the assistant manager, had told her about the restaurant: Whopper® Junior, for here or to go? Small, medium, or large? It was different from cooking at home because most of the food was already made, and she just cooked it. At home, she prepared everything from scratch, and she was a good cook.

It was a lot to remember, but Linda assured her that after one or two days, everything would be easy. She was grateful that the kitchen area where she worked was small but well organized. Other people were responsible for looking at the computer screen and putting the orders together on the trays or in take-out bags. She just had to cook the burgers and fries and assemble the salads. *"We're really busy from 11:30 to 1:00 for the lunch crowd, so be ready!"* Linda told her.

When Flor opened her apartment door, she was shocked again by the emptiness. For a few hours at the restaurant, she forgot about Ricardo. Now, with Betina at Maria's house, there was nothing for Flor to do but go to bed. She folded one of Maria's blankets to make a mattress, put her sweater under her head for a pillow, and pulled another blanket over her. She closed her eyes.

The questions started again, but this time they were about Betina. Who could take care of her while Flor was at work? Maria wouldn't do it. Would Maria's mom, Flor's mother-in-law? She would ask in the morning.

Flor couldn't ask her brother, Felipe; she just couldn't. He only lived two miles away, but how could she tell him that Ricardo had left her and Betina? He would blame it all on her. Maybe it was her fault.

"What did I do to make Ricardo leave us and find someone else?" she wondered. *"Was he tired of me? Am I ugly? Were there clues that Ricardo was unhappy with me, enough to leave me for another woman?"*

Ricardo worked a lot of overtime and sometimes slept at the homes of friends close to the job site. Had he really been with the other woman then?

"I can't tell Felipe, and I definitely can't tell my parents," she thought. *"They'll tell me to come back home. Is Maria right that there is no place here for Betina and me? And how can I call Ricardo and hear him tell me he is never coming home?"*

Her stomach began to hurt. She rubbed it. Flor needed to sleep. She had so many things to do in the morning. Finally, she rolled over and tried to relax.

The next thing Flor knew the sun was streaming in the window. She felt tired. She took a shower to wake up and got dressed. She needed to buy some food, but that would have to wait. First things first: get a cup of coffee and pick up Betina.

Betina answered the door when Flor rang the bell at Maria's house. She jumped into her mother's arms.

"Mama! You're here. Come see Grandma. She made me hot chocolate and tortillas for breakfast."

"That sounds delicious." Betina led Flor into the kitchen. Maria was sitting at the kitchen table. Her mother, Magdalena (Lena for short), was standing at the stove stirring the hot chocolate. She was shorter and rounder than her daughter. Her dark, silver-streaked hair was pulled back into a bun. She turned around when Flor came into the room.

"Flor. How good to see you! It is so nice to have Betina back. I missed you both when you were away. How is your family?"

Flor's eyes filled with tears. *"It's wonderful to see you, too. My parents are fine. We had a great trip. The time passed so quickly, and now we're home."*

No one said anything for a minute. Then Lena said, *"Here, sit down, and have some hot chocolate. Or do you want coffee?"*

"Coffee, please. Thanks."

"Maria tells me you have a job. What are you doing?"

Flor explained all about it.

"Mama, you are going to work? Can I come with you?" Betina asked.

"No, Little One. There isn't anything for you to do there. And I'll be working very hard."

"What are you going to do with Betina, Flor?" Maria asked. *"You can't leave her here. We are too busy."*

"Maria," said her mother. *"You may be too busy, but I'm not. Betina can stay here with me. I love taking care of her. She is no trouble. She can help me make tamales for Mexican Independence Day."*

Flor looked at her mother-in-law. *"Are you sure? It would really help. My shift is from 11:00 to 7:00. I was so worried about what to do. It will only be for a week. I'm sure I can find something more permanent for her."*

"You take your time. I know things are hard and confusing right now," Lena said.

Was this kind, helpful, and caring person really Ricardo and Maria's mother?

"Come here, Betina," Flor said. Betina climbed up into her mother's lap. *"Grandma says you can stay here with her this week. She needs your help to make tamales for September 16th. That's Mexican Independence Day. Do you remember?"*

"Is that when they have the Mexican dancers and singers and the parade downtown?" Betina asked.

"Yes, that's it."

"Can we go now?"

The adults, even Maria, laughed. *"No, Little One. We love it, too. But it's still almost two weeks away."*

Flor continued, *"I have to go now so I can get to work on time. You be good for Grandma and Aunt Maria, Betina. I'll come over or call tomorrow and tell you about the job. Good-bye. I love you."*

"I love you, too, Mama," she said and gave her a hug and a kiss.

Maria, Lena, and Betina walked Flor to the door.

"Thank you again, so much," Flor said.

"It's a pleasure," said Lena. *"Don't worry about a thing. We'll be fine. We'll talk to you tomorrow."*

Flor hugged them all and waved good-bye.

Maria and Lena lived a few blocks beyond the bus stop in front of the school. Flor started home. She looked at the school as she walked by. It was such a pretty old building. She could tell that people had pride in it and took care of it. She was just about to cross the street when she noticed a big blue-and-white banner hanging on the fence in front of the school. It wasn't there yesterday. She read it. In both Spanish and English it said, "Now Enrolling—Pre-school."

Now Enrolling
Pre-school

Flor looked at her watch. She still had some time until she had to be at work. Quickly, she walked into the school. A sign on the wall said Office and had an arrow pointing down the hall.

Flor paused at the door to the office. Two boys were sitting on a bench. There were several people behind the counter, but they were all busy on the telephone or at the computer or filing drawers. Finally, the woman at the front desk looked up from her papers and smiled at Flor.

"Can I help you?" she asked in English.

Flor shook her head. "No English," she said.

The woman, still smiling, called to a Hispanic woman who was working at another desk.

"Hello. Can I help you?" the second woman asked Flor in Spanish.

"Yes. I saw the sign out on the fence that you are enrolling children for pre-school classes. I have a daughter who is four years old. Can she come to the class?"

"She is the right age. It's for four-year-olds. But you need to fill out these papers, bring in her immunization record and birth certificate, and then the teacher will look them over. Do you have her records?"

"Yes," said Flor. *"But she never gets sick."*

"That's good," said the woman. *"But we still need to make sure she's had all her shots so that she doesn't get sick when she starts school."* The woman

handed her one more paper. *"These are the hours. There are still openings in the class, but the program doesn't start until next week. It meets Monday through Friday from 12:50 until 3:30."*

Flor took the paper. *"Thank you. Do I have to fill out the forms now?"*

"You can, if you want to. You can sit at the table out in the hall."

Flor thought quickly. *"Can I take them home with me and bring everything back in a day or two?"*

"Certainly. And are you interested in this, too?" The woman handed Flor a flier that said "Free English Classes for Adults." One side was written in English, and the other side was in Spanish.

"I am very interested in the classes. Where are they? And when are they?" Flor asked.

"They are here at the school in a room upstairs. The classes are every Monday, Wednesday, and Thursday morning at 9:00 AM for two hours."

"Oh, but the hours for the pre-school class are different," said Flor. She was disappointed.

"Don't worry. You can bring your daughter, too. There is someone to take care of the young children while the adults have their class. Our teacher is excellent. We are very lucky to have the program."

"You have a baby-sitter. That's good. What is the cost?" asked Flor.

The woman smiled. *"That's the best part. The class is free."*

"How do I sign up?"

"Come Monday morning, and wait in the front lobby. The teacher comes to get everyone, and they all go to class together. She has registration papers."

"I just got a job, and I start at 11:00. . . ."

"You can talk to the teacher. I'm sure she can accommodate that."

Flor thanked the woman. Everyone was so friendly, even though she didn't speak English. She wondered why Ricardo always said she didn't need to learn English. She thought he was protecting her from bad people, but the people she talked to at school and Burger King were nice. Ricardo was the bad one.

Flor glanced at the clock on the office wall. She had time to go home, change into the uniform she got yesterday, and get to Burger King before her shift started. So much was happening!

CHAPTER 4

After her shift, Flor didn't really feel like going home. Why go there? There was no one to talk to, no Betina to hug and care for. She stayed at Burger King for a few minutes to talk to Linda.

"You are a good worker, Flor," said Linda. *"You learn fast. You'll do well here."*

Flor felt shy about this praise, but she also felt proud.

"This is my first job," she said.

"I know," said Linda. *"That's why I am surprised at how well you are doing. Now, go home! You must be very tired."*

Flor got her bag and walked out the door. The night was a little chilly. *"Winter will come soon,"* she thought. *"I will have to pay for heating the apartment."* Flor realized she needed to figure out whether she and Betina could survive on her earnings. If Ricardo never came back, she would have all the responsibility for rent, food, clothing, and bills. She returned to Denver from Mexico with $100 in her purse, but the taxi ride and food and other necessities had already used half of that. She and

Betina had $50 until Flor got her first paycheck. That was not enough.

Flor arrived home. She got out a pencil and some paper and sat down on her blankets. She wrote down all the things she needed money for. Next to each thing, she wrote how much she thought it would cost. Before she left for Mexico, it was her responsibility to pay the bills. Ricardo gave her the money, and she went to the market to get money orders and make the payments. She knew how much to estimate.

Flor was in the middle of this when there was a loud knock on her front door. Flor looked up. Ricardo, she thought. But no, he had a key. He would just come in.

"Who is it?"

"Flor, it's me, Felipe!"

Flor jumped to her feet and rushed to the door. For a moment she forgot that she didn't want to see her brother. Here was a member of her own family. She threw open the door.

"Felipe!" She hugged him enthusiastically.

"My God, Flor, you had us so worried! Mama and Papa did not hear from you. Why didn't you call me when you arrived in Denver? We couldn't reach you by telephone, and I came over earlier but you weren't here!" Felipe stopped talking. *"Wait. Flor, are you moving?"*

Flor looked behind her at the empty apartment.

"No—"

Felipe walked around the apartment. *"What is going on here?"*

Shame filled Flor. Quietly, she said, *"Ricardo left me. He took everything. I don't even know where he is."*

"Everything? Betina, too?"

Flor was shocked at this suggestion. *"Oh, no! Betina is with Lena! She is staying with Lena for a few days until I can find someone to care for her while I work."*

"You left Betina with Lena? How could you? What if she gives her to Ricardo?"

Felipe didn't seem very surprised at the news that Ricardo was gone. Did he know about the other woman? How many people kept this secret from her? Shame, now anger, took hold of Flor.

"She won't do that."

"How do you know? She might even keep Betina for herself. You should have called me. I am your brother."

Flor knew Lena would not keep Betina from her. Lena was the only one who was kind to Flor. Maria was cold and distant.

Flor sat down on her blankets and put her face in her hands. Without raising her head, she said, *"Felipe, did you know Ricardo had another family?"*

Felipe didn't answer. Flor looked at him. His face was red.

"I thought maybe he did," he said. He sat down

next to her on the folded blankets. *"I asked him once why he was gone so many nights each week."*

"What did he say?"

"He got mad. He said, 'Mind your own business!'"

Felipe and Flor were silent for a few moments. Finally, Felipe spoke. *"You must come home with me."*

Flor didn't want to go home with her brother. He lived in a little house with his girlfriend and two men she didn't know. It was not a good place for a small child. It was not a good place for her. This apartment, even with no furniture, was better.

"I have a job, Felipe. I can keep the apartment."

"You have no furniture! You are alone! You need my help. You need your family."

Flor knew what he said was true.

"Yes, I need your help," she said. *"But you live close by, and you can lend me some furniture. I'll call Ricardo, too. Betina is his daughter, and he will help me take care of her."*

Flor said this with confidence, but she did not feel confident.

Felipe shook his head. *"No. You have to get Betina back from Lena right away. You must never leave her with Ricardo's family. They'll take her away. And you can't afford rent, food, and a babysitter for Betina."*

Flor and Felipe talked and argued for a long time. Finally, Flor said, *"Felipe, I will call Ricardo. If he gives me some money for a baby-sitter for Betina and gives me some furniture, will you agree with me?"*

Felipe said, *"OK, but call Ricardo tomorrow. You must not leave Betina with Lena all week. I'll be back tomorrow night."*

Flor walked to the door with her brother. As she opened it for him, he said, *"Don't worry, Flor. Everything will be alright. I never liked Ricardo anyway."*

Flor almost laughed, but she was afraid laughter would bring tears. Now he was telling her he didn't like her husband. Why didn't anyone tell her about Ricardo before?

"Goodnight, Felipe," she said.

After he left, Flor went back to her figures. Her paycheck would be about $1,280 per month, before taxes. She thought taxes might be about $200. Her rent was $600. That left about $480 for everything else. Other expenses that she was sure about were bus fare, heat, electricity, food, and telephone. She estimated the cost of a baby-sitter, but she didn't even know if she could find one she would trust with her precious child. When she added it all up, she saw she would not have enough money for everything. Even without a telephone, she would not have enough.

If Ricardo did not help her, she and Betina would have to move in with Felipe. His house was so small. He and his girlfriend had one bedroom. His roommates paid rent for their bedroom, so

Betina and Flor would sleep in the living room. They would have no privacy. Felipe would expect Flor to cook and clean for everyone.

"I don't want to move in with Felipe!" she thought. *"Ricardo has to give me $400 a month for a baby-sitter. I'll make him give me money."*

Suddenly, she realized that she assumed Ricardo was gone forever. Did she want him to return? Should she call and say, *"Ricardo, give me money,"* or should she call and say, *"Ricardo, come back to us!"*?

Flor took off her uniform and hung it carefully in the closet. She wrapped herself in a sweater and lay down on her bed of blankets. She was so tired that it felt soft and warm, and she fell asleep at once.

Early the next morning, Flor hurried out to the pay phone on the corner. She called the telephone number Maria gave her for Ricardo. He answered on the first ring.

"Hello?" he said, in a quiet voice.

"Ricardo?" Flor said.

"Yes," he said.

Flor's heart beat hard against her chest. *"Ricardo, this is me."*

Silence. Cars drove by, and a small wind blew trash into the street. Then Ricardo said, *"Flor?"*

"Yes."

"Who gave you this number? You cannot call me here."

Flor wanted to cry. Was he worried about his new wife? Did she know about Flor and Betina? Or, was he lying to another woman, too?

"I need to talk to you," she said.

"Why?"

At that moment, Flor could not think of one good reason. It was hard to breathe. She thought she was going to faint. Betina, Betina, she said to herself. She forced herself to say, *"We have to talk about Betina."*

"Call me later," said Ricardo. *"Call me at about 6:00 this evening. Then I can talk."*

"Wait. . . ."

Ricardo hung up, and Flor was left holding the phone in her hand. All her questions returned. Why did you leave us? Are you coming back? Will you help us? Didn't you love me? Don't you love your daughter?

An automated voice came over the phone: "If you'd like to make a call, please hang up and try again."

All day Flor worried about the bad conversation she had with Ricardo. Even that morning when she saw Betina, with her happy talk and smiling face, she could not forget. She was suspicious of Lena, too, because of what Felipe said. Was he right? She had watched her mother-in-law and Betina carefully. Was Lena trying to steal Betina?

At work, Flor made several small mistakes. She

made too many Whopper Juniors and no Whoppers, and she spilled a container of french fries.

"You seem distracted," said Linda. *"Take your break."*

But Flor didn't want to take her break until 6:00, when she planned to call Ricardo. *"No, no, everything is OK,"* she told Linda. She tried to erase her worries from her mind and concentrate on her work. She could not care for Betina if she lost her job.

Finally, the time came to make the call. She didn't want anyone to hear, so she went outside to the pay phone, deposited 50 cents, and punched in the number.

"What do you want, Flor?" said Ricardo. He didn't even greet her.

She forgot what she was going to say.

"I. . . . you. . . . you took everything!"

Ricardo immediately became angry. *"What did you expect? You left me. Was I supposed to leave all our things in an empty apartment?"*

"I left you? Oh, Ricardo, how can you say that? I told you I was only going for a visit to see my parents. I told you I would be back in September. When I returned, you were gone! And you took everything. I need some of it, and money for a baby-sitter for Betina."

"I knew it! I knew you were calling to ask for money. That's all you care about."

Flor took a deep breath. This conversation was

not going the way she planned. She wanted to be calm and reasonable and not get angry.

"No, Ricardo, I care about our daughter. I care about you, my husband. I want to know if you are coming back."

Ricardo coughed. *"That is difficult. I have new responsibilities."*

"You are my husband."

"Not really," said Ricardo. *"We never got a marriage license. I have a real wife now. And she's not going to Mexico for months and leaving me alone."*

Flor felt like Ricardo had kicked her in the stomach. It was more difficult to hear the truth from him than she thought it would be.

"Then you are not coming back?" she asked softly.

"No."

"What about Betina?"

"She seems fine. She was happy to see me."

Flor panicked. *"What do you mean? When did you see her?"*

"At my mother's house. I went there today after work. She looks happy with my mom."

"That is a temporary arrangement," said Flor. *"I found a school for her, and I'm looking for a baby-sitter for the time that I'm at work."*

"If you leave her with my mom, you won't need a baby-sitter."

"I'm not leaving her with your mother! She will live with me."

"She can live with you on the weekends. That way, I can stop and see her at my mom's after work every day. I can take her to meet her new mother."

"New mother? She only has one mother! Me!" Flor began to cry a little. Felipe was right. Ricardo had the furniture, most of her belongings, and now he wanted Betina, too.

Ricardo's voice got ugly. *"Listen, Flor. I have been patient with you. When you walked out with my daughter and left me alone for so long, I paid the rent on the apartment, even though I don't live there. You have a place to stay until the end of the month. I have been fair. It was my hard work that earned the money for everything we bought for the apartment. It's mine. If you want Betina to live with you, find a way without my help. I have a nice family for her."*

Quietly, Flor hung up the telephone. She wiped her eyes. Now, there were no more questions. She went inside and finished her shift. Then, even though it was late, she went to Lena's and got her little girl out of bed. Lena tried to stop her, but Flor knew what she had to do.

When Felipe knocked on the apartment door, she was ready.

"You were right," she said. *"Let's go."*

CHAPTER 5

My Journal, Thursday, September 20

I am so happy to be in the English class. I will work hard and learn much English. I like my job and I want to do better.

Karen, Flor's English teacher, translated Flor's journal entry into English, and wrote a response. Then she moved on to the next student. Flor reread everything. English was difficult. Even when Flor used the dictionary, most Spanish words had so many different meanings in English that she didn't know which one to choose. And her attempts at translating English sentences into Spanish often made no scnsc. But it made her feel good to read what her teacher wrote:

Karen:

I know how hard it is to learn a new language, but little by little you will get better. I am very happy that you are in the class. Thank you for coming.

This class was so different from Flor's school in Mexico. The room was bright and cheerful. It was big. It had a space at one end for the childcare worker and the children. Betina was shy at first, but soon joined in the games and art projects with the other children.

Flor turned to the woman sitting next to her. Carmen was from Argentina. They met just three days before on Flor's first day in class, but it seemed like they had known each other for years. Carmen was older than Flor. She was the mother of two children, a boy and a girl. It was her second year in class, and she asked a lot of questions and made jokes all the time. She made Karen and all the students laugh.

"Do you want to go out for coffee tomorrow morning since we don't have class? We can meet before I go to work," Flor said.

"Sure. How about at 9:00? I have to bring my son to school then. We can go over to the bagel shop."

"OK. Great."

The teacher interrupted their conversation. "Let's talk about September 16th, Mexican Independence Day."

Flor had to leave class a few minutes early each day to get to work on time. At 10:50 she put her journal and notebook into her bag, excused herself, got Betina, and went downstairs. Lena was waiting for her outside. This was the hardest part of the day for Flor. Over the weekend, she realized that she didn't know anyone who could care for Betina while she was at work except her mother-in-law. Felipe and his girlfriend both had jobs. Even after what her brother had said about Ricardo taking Betina, Flor still felt that Lena loved them both. *"Lena won't let Ricardo take Betina,"* she thought. But they might get too attached to each other, and she was very worried about what Ricardo might do. If Ricardo could take all their furniture and marry another woman, he could easily lie to Lena. Would Lena know if he lied, and could she stop Ricardo from taking Betina?

"Hi, Lena. Thank you for helping us."

"I'm happy to do it. We're having fun together. Betina's class is this afternoon at 12:50, right?"

Flor said, *"Right. Then you pick her up at 3:30, and I'll come to your house to get her as soon as I can after work."*

Lena didn't respond. She wanted her granddaughter to stay with her, but she didn't want to interfere with Flor and Ricardo's problems.

"Bye, Little One. I'll see you tonight."

"Bye, Mama. I love you."

The shift seemed to pass quickly. Flor had a late lunch. She bought a Whopper and fries at half price and had her second free drink. She ate quickly and went back to work before her break was over so she could leave on time to get Betina.

It was late when Betina and Flor got to Felipe's house. Music was blaring from one bedroom. The

TV was on and nobody was watching it. Felipe's girlfriend was on the phone.

"I'm sleepy," said Betina.

"OK, Little One. I'm tired, too," said Flor. *"I'll make the bed."*

Flor put some sheets on the couch in the living room. She helped Betina take off her clothes and brush her teeth. She helped her get under the covers on the couch.

"Mama, it's noisy here," Betina whined. *"I want to go to sleep."*

Flor turned off the TV and knocked on the bedroom door.

"Yeah?" said the man who rented the room. He didn't open the door.

"Excuse me," said Flor. *"My daughter and I are going to sleep. Will you turn the music down?"*

The man said something Flor didn't hear. It didn't sound nice. Then he turned down the music a little.

"Thank you," said Flor. Once again, she felt like crying. Where was Felipe? She didn't want to be in this house with his girlfriend. She didn't want to be there with this strange man with the loud music. She didn't want to be there at all. Once again, she remembered Betina. She must not cry. Betina must not see how sad and angry and lonely Flor was.

She got in bed with Betina. She cuddled up to her warm little daughter and sang soft songs until Betina was asleep. Flor stayed awake for a long time, listening to the music and the sound of Felipe's girlfriend chatting on the phone.

The next morning, Flor and Betina met Carmen and her daughter Rosy by the flagpole. They all walked across the street to the bagel shop. They got a table outside and sat down. The girls were happy sharing a muffin while Carmen and Flor talked.

"What do you think of our English class?" Flor asked.

"I love it. And it's different from last year. Now there are people from all over the world. Last year we had mostly Spanish speakers."

"But don't you feel lost when Karen speaks all in English?"

"Sometimes. It's very difficult at the beginning. What she says is true. Little by little we do learn English. If she speaks in Spanish, we don't try as hard to understand. And with so many people speaking other languages that Karen doesn't know, it's not fair to them for her to use Spanish with us."

Flor answered, *"You're right. I'm glad I can write my journal in Spanish, though."*

"You'll be surprised. Before long, you'll be writing most of it in English." Carmen smiled at Flor. *"Karen is very curious. I tell her everything in my* journal." She said "journal" in English. She sounded just like Karen, and Flor laughed.

"Where were all the students who came yesterday? It seems like different people come to every class."

Carmen answered, *"Some people have to work or have doctor appointments. Sometimes cold weather keeps people away. Karen is a good teacher, and she knows that people come when they can."* Carmen paused. *"You look tired, Flor."*

"I am. It's been a hard week. I started my job and English classes, and Betina started pre-school, and. . . ."

Suddenly, she was telling Carmen about everything that had happened since she came back from Mexico. About the empty apartment and Ricardo leaving, and Maria being so unfriendly, and Lena being wonderful. About Felipe's warning that Ricardo could take Betina. About getting her job and finding the ESL and pre-school classes. And about her money worries, living in Felipe's house, and trusting Lena to watch Betina. Everything. Carmen was a good listener.

"We went to bed very late," said Flor. *"It's awful for us at Felipe's house. My brother cares about us, but it's different here than in Mexico. I'm trying to save up money to get a place of our own, but it's so expensive. The worst part is having Betina go to my mother-in-law's house. Lena is wonderful, but her daughter is very unfriendly now, and I'm really scared about what Ricardo might do. I know he sees Betina almost every day over there, and I don't trust him. He told me he wants to take her to meet her new mother!"*

Carmen said, *"That's a man for you. They're*

never satisfied. Listen, it's only 9:45. The girls are restless. Let's walk around for a little while."

"OK."

They threw away their trash and started walking down the street.

"I've been talking this whole time, Carmen. Tell me about you and your family. How long have you been in Denver?"

Carmen answered, *"Three years. We're from Buenos Aires. There was no work for my husband there. His aunt and uncle and their family live here in Denver. His uncle manages a warehouse, and now my husband works there, too. We lived with them when we first came here, but when we had our second child, it was too crowded. Our apartment isn't very nice, but the rent is low. Someday we want to buy a house."*

"I used to dream about that, too," said Flor. *"Now I just want to find a good baby-sitter for Betina and save enough money to move out of my brother's place."*

"In Argentina I was a secretary," said Carmen. *"I liked it very much. I made a lot of money, and I went dancing every weekend. Do you like to dance?"*

"Yes," said Flor.

"Oh, me, too. Then I met Mario, and I fell in love. He doesn't want me to get a job," Carmen said. *"Sometimes I watch my neighbor's baby. Rosy likes that. She misses her brother when he is at school."*

Flor said, *"Betina gets lonely, too. Sometimes I think it's harder to have one child than two."*

Carmen nodded in agreement and then said, *"Betina and Rosy seem to like each other. Can Betina come to our apartment to play one day?"*

"That sounds like a good idea."

Flor realized it was getting late. She had to take Betina back to school to meet Lena and then go to work. She turned to her daughter.

"Betina, we have to go. Say good-bye to Rosy."

Betina grabbed her new friend's hand. *"Oh, Mama, can Rosy come, too?"*

"Not this time, Little One," Flor said, smiling.

Carmen said, *"Look at them! They're so cute."* She paused. *"You know, Flor, maybe I could baby-sit. It would give Rosy and me something to do to bring Betina to pre-school, and we have to come back at 3:30 anyway for my son. We only live three blocks away. I need to talk it over with my husband, but I'm sure he'll think it's fine."*

Flor was astonished. She and Carmen felt comfortable with each other from the beginning, but they were still almost strangers. Would this be a wise decision? Who could she ask to help her decide? She couldn't think of anyone.

"Thank you. Everything is happening so fast. I need time to think. Can I call you over the weekend and let you know?"

"Sure. No problem. Here's my phone number." She wrote her number on a scrap of paper and gave

it to Flor. *"It's not the answer to all your problems. Maybe we can try it out and see how it goes for a week."*

"I'll think about it," said Flor.

The two women said good-bye to each other and went in opposite directions.

Flor could see Lena waiting for them in front of the school. But today she wasn't alone. Flor felt her stomach tighten.

"Papa!" Betina shouted as she ran up to him. Ricardo lifted his daughter up in the air. She laughed happily.

As Flor watched them, she had to admit to herself that Ricardo was a good father. Clearly, he and Betina loved each other. She knew it would not be good for Betina to grow up without him. She wanted to believe that Ricardo thought she, Flor, was a good mother. *"He won't take our daughter away from me,"* she thought.

Lena walked over to Flor and said, *"Ricardo came over for an early lunch. He has to get back to work soon. Betina can help me make tamales for Independence Day. She'll be tired when you come to pick her up tonight."*

Flor felt reassured. *"OK. I'll see you tonight."*

Flor turned and walked over to Ricardo and Betina.

"Hello, Ricardo."

He still held Betina in his arms. Flor looked into his face.

"He is a handsome man," Flor thought. *"The three of us should be going home together, to our own apartment. Oh, what happened to change Ricardo's mind? I know he loved me."*

Ricardo answered in a low voice without emotion, *"Hello, Flor."*

Flor said to her daughter, *"I have to hurry and get to work. I'll pick you up at Grandma's tonight, Little One. I love you."*

"I love you, too, Mama. Bye."

Flor walked quickly away.

Work was busy, as usual, but Flor continued thinking about her problems. Carmen's offer to baby-sit was unexpected, but it could save her. On the other hand, she didn't want to deny her mother-in-law or Ricardo the chance to be in Betina's life. What did the future hold for Flor? Things could never be the way they once were. Flor didn't want to be bitter and angry with Ricardo, not only for her daughter's sake, but also for her own. She was not an angry person who wanted to hurt others. She didn't want Betina to be like that either. Somchow . . . .

"Flor, this order is for large fries, not regular."

"Sorry," said Flor.

At her break, Linda sat down with her.

"Flor, you're making too many mistakes. Some of the other employees are complaining. Is something wrong?"

"Family problems," said Flor. She looked down at the table. *"I'm so sorry. I'll try to do better."*

Linda reached her hand across the table and touched Flor's arm. *"You're a good, hard worker. I know it's difficult to stop worrying about things just because you're at work. This is what I do. When I get to work, I put on my hat. The only thoughts I allow myself while I'm wearing my hat are work thoughts. It's a way to take a break from my problems. Try it."*

"OK," said Flor. She felt bad. Linda was being nice, but Flor knew Linda was warning her to pay more attention, or she would lose her job.

CHAPTER 6

My Journal, Monday, September 24

Today I tire. All the weekend I look apartment. I walk in all place, but no. *My doter and me go celebramos 16 de Septiembre* downtown.

Karen:

I know how difficult it is to find an apartment in the neighborhood. If I hear of one I will tell you. Thank you for writing so much English today!

For regular verbs we add "ed" to make the past tense. Examples are "looked" and "walked." Try that next time.

While Karen was reading other journal entries, Flor turned to Carmen and whispered, *"I'm exhausted. I looked all over the neighborhood for an apartment, and the cheapest rent I found was $700."*

"Have you thought about my offer to baby-sit? It's fine with my husband."

Flor was glad to hear Carmen repeat her offer. She nodded. *"Yes. I accept. And thank you. Thank you very much."*

Carmen was delighted. *"Great!"*

Karen looked over at the two women. "You two seem happy," she said, smiling.

Carmen nodded. "I baby-sit her."

"You're going to baby-sit Flor?"

"Yes."

"She's a grown woman! She doesn't need a baby-sitter."

"No! I going to baby-sit her girl, Betina," said Carmen.

"You're going to baby-sit *for* Flor?" asked Karen.

"Yes, of course," said Carmen.

Senem, a small Turkish woman, spoke up. "That's good. You are friends. Here in America is hard, because we have not our family to help with children. I am missing my mother and sisters."

"Let's talk about families," said Karen. She showed them how to make family trees. When they were done, she said, "Tomorrow, bring in photographs of your families."

After class, Flor put $30 into Carmen's hand.

"It's not much," she said. *"But right now, this is all I can afford. Can Betina come tomorrow? I will tell Lena tonight."*

"Oh, Flor, don't pay me now," said Carmen.

"Wait until you have worked a little longer. I don't need the extra money immediately."

Flor smiled at Carmen's generosity. *"No,"* she said. *"It's better if I pay you right from the start. Then we won't have bad feelings about anything."*

Carmen closed her hand on the money. *"Are you sure?"* she asked. *"I can take $20 a week."*

"Thirty dollars. And, yes, I am sure."

"Listen, Flor, when we spoke last week, something you said didn't sound right. You said that you and Ricardo never really got married. Now Ricardo says he really is married to this new woman, right?"

"Right."

"I looked up marriage on the Internet. In Colorado there's something called a common law marriage. If you live together for a long time and say you're married, then the law says you are married. You don't have to have a ceremony or even have a marriage license."

"Really?" asked Flor.

"Yes. And, I found out that it's illegal to be married to two women. It's called bigamy."

"So, Ricardo is breaking the law?"

"I think so," said Carmen. *"The rat."*

Flor thanked Carmen for the information. *"I have to go now. Let's talk later,"* she said.

Lena was waiting outside for Betina, and Flor wished she could tell her about the new babysitting arrangement, but she knew she would need time to explain everything. She said hello to Lena and good-bye to Betina and hurried off to work.

She felt almost normal for the first time in the two weeks since she had been back in Denver. Carmen was going to be a true friend. She seemed to be really pleased to be taking care of Betina. How kind of her to look up all that information on the Internet! Flor didn't know how she would use it, but it might be helpful.

Flor thought about the Turkish woman, Senem. She seemed nice. Flor liked her. She was very friendly and spoke good English, like Carmen. *"Maybe she'll be my friend, too,"* thought Flor. *"She is lonely."*

Flor had a good day. She concentrated on her work and didn't make any mistakes. Both Linda and David complimented her. During her break David sat with her, and they talked about her childhood in Mexico and his in the United States. They discovered that their grandparents were from the same small town. *"But my grandparents moved to the United States,"* said David, *"and yours stayed in Mexico."*

David stood up to go back to work. *"I know you take care of your daughter on the weekend, but we have some Saturday hours available. If you want to work extra, let me know."*

"Thank you. If I can, I will."

After work, Flor hummed as she walked to the

bus stop. The evening air felt clean and crisp. On the bus, she began to get a little nervous. She must tell Lena about Carmen in a way that would not hurt Lena's feelings or make her mad. Lena was kind and helpful. Flor thought carefully about what she would say.

When she arrived at the stop near Lena's house, her good mood disappeared. Her hands shook, and her forehead was wet with sweat.

"This is not the hardest thing I have done," she told herself. *"Getting a job was harder. Calling Ricardo was more difficult."* She walked quickly, trying to release some of her nervous energy.

Betina flew into Flor's arms when she saw her.

"Mama! We had chicken for dinner. What did you have?"

Flor kissed Betina and hugged her. She smelled delicious, like shampoo and lotion. *"I didn't have dinner. I think I'll just eat you."*

"No, I don't taste good!"

"You certainly smell good. Did you have a bath?" asked Flor.

"Yes, a bubble bath. Grandma has purple bubble bath soap!"

"Oh, that's why you're purple."

"I am not!" Betina giggled.

They talked and joked for a minute more, and then Flor settled Betina in front of a cartoon on television.

"I need to talk to Grandma," she said.

Betina yawned and cuddled her doll close to her. *"We're sleepy,"* she said. *"We want to spend the night here."*

"No, we're going home."

"I don't want to go there. It's noisy. I can sleep with Grandma in her bed, and Aunt Maria will sing to me in the morning. I'm not going back to Uncle Felipe's house."

"That's where we live. You don't have a choice," said Flor. She tried not to be cross, but she didn't want to have this argument with Betina now, with all that she needed to say to Lena.

"You go. My dolly and I are staying here."

"No, you are not."

"YES, WE ARE."

Flor stared at her stubborn little daughter. A flush of anger spread across her face. Lena came into the living room.

"She'll be asleep in a few minutes," whispered Lena. *"She's tired. Just leave her there for now."*

"OK. I can carry her home," said Flor. *"I need to talk to you about something, anyway. Let's go into the kitchen."*

Lena pulled out two chairs from the table. Both women sat down. *"What is it?"* asked Lena.

"Thank you for all your help with Betina, and with, with everything."

Lena smiled. *"It's my pleasure."*

"Well, now your life can return to normal. I found someone who will take care of Betina while I am at

work. She's a woman in my English class. She has a daughter, so Betina will have someone to play with. And Ricardo can spend time with Betina on the weekend."

The look on Lena's face told Flor that Lena did not think this was good news.

"What have I done to make you unhappy?" she asked. *"I have been good to Betina. Why are you doing this?"*

"I am not unhappy with you!" Flor reached across the table and took Lena's hand. *"You have been wonderful! I know you love Betina. It's. . . . I'm . . . . I am afraid of Ricardo. Of what Ricardo might do."*

There. She said it.

Lena pulled her hand away from Flor's hand. *"Ricardo won't hurt Betina,"* she said.

"No, no, of course not. I'm not worried about that." Flor struggled to explain what she meant. *"Ricardo threatened to take Betina to live with him and his new family."*

"What? How can he do that?"

"He says he has a nice family for her. He says he has a new mother for her. He says if I make any trouble for him, he will take her."

"Why didn't you tell me? This is not right. Ricardo should not use Betina to make you do what he wants you to do."

Flor began to talk. She told Lena how frightening it was to walk into an empty apartment. *"I thought Ricardo was hurt or dead!"* she said. She told Lena everything Ricardo said, how he accused her of leaving him, how he told her not to ask him for money.

Lena listened quietly. Sometimes she asked a question. Finally, Flor was finished. Lena now knew Flor's side of the story.

"I'm sorry, Flor," said Lena, quietly. *"I knew Ricardo wasn't telling me everything, but I was trying not to get in the middle of your problems. Of course you must take Betina to Carmen, if that makes you feel better."*

Both women were silent for a minute.

"Can Betina spend the night with me sometimes?" asked Lena.

"Of course!" said Flor. *"I want you to be in her life. She loves you."*

"I love her, too." Lena paused. *"If you need help with anything, with money, or with furniture, please ask me."*

"Thank you. Right now I'm trying to save some money for an apartment, but they are so expensive."

Lena stood up. *"I'm going to call Ricardo right now,"* she said. *"He is going to come over here and talk with you."*

Ricardo didn't argue with Lena, and he arrived quickly. He kissed his mother on the cheek and sat down across from Flor at the kitchen table.

"You two need to talk, face to face. I'll be in my bedroom with Betina," said Lena. She left, giving Flor a little nod as she went.

It was difficult to talk to Ricardo. He seemed to be a stranger, not her husband, the man Flor was married to for five years. His eyes were cold, and his face was closed. Flor started the conversation by telling him what Carmen said about Colorado marriage laws and bigamy. She didn't threaten him, but she could see that he understood that it was illegal to be "married" to two women.

Once he muttered, *"Who have you been talking to?"* He didn't deny what she said, though.

"He knew about this all the time," she thought.

Then she told him that Carmen would be babysitting Betina.

Ricardo looked tired and annoyed. *"How can I be a father to Betina if she is not at my mother's house?"*

"You can come to Felipe's house and get her on Sundays."

"That's not convenient! My family goes to church and has a big meal on Sundays. I can't just leave early and go get Betina."

Although the words "my family" were like a slap in her face, Flor showed no emotion. *"Then you can have her on Saturdays."*

Ricardo grumbled about this, too, but finally agreed. *"Felipe and I don't like each other,"* he said.

"I don't want to go inside his house. You can meet me outside."

"Call before you come, then," said Flor. *"Betina will be ready."*

"You've changed," said Ricardo as he left. Flor couldn't tell what he meant. Was it a compliment or an insult?

"Whose fault is that?" she asked. She wished she could take the harsh words back as soon as they were out of her mouth.

Ricardo didn't answer but raised his eyebrows at her and walked down the street to his car. She watched him go. She recognized his walk. She was familiar with his body, but she felt as if she did not know this man, the father of her child, at all anymore.

He was already out of sight when she realized that she forgot to ask him for money. How could she ask a stranger for money? *"For Betina,"* she told herself, as usual. *"Next time, I must ask for money for Betina."*

As the weeks passed, Flor, Betina, and Ricardo settled into a routine. Ricardo called and then came to get Betina on Saturdays. He didn't like picking Betina up at Felipe's house. Felipe always came to the door and stared at him in an unfriendly manner. As soon as Ricardo and Betina left, Flor hurried to work. She was trying to make some extra money for an apartment.

The weather grew colder, the days became shorter, and the trees lost their leaves. Flor's coat was one of the few things Ricardo left in the apartment, but Betina was too big for her old winter clothes. Ricardo surprised Flor by taking Betina shopping and buying her a winter coat and some sweaters. At those times, when he did something nice for Betina, Flor almost liked Ricardo. But usually when she saw him, she felt odd. Who was he? She still could not make herself ask this stranger for money.

CHAPTER 7

"Why are you trying to make things hard for me? Every Saturday it's the same, the ugly look, the silence! I should wipe the floor with your face . . . ."

Ricardo was shouting at Felipe. Flor was in the bathroom getting Betina ready for her visit with Ricardo. She heard the argument and told Betina to stay in the bathroom. She ran to the front door. Felipe and Ricardo were standing outside. Their faces were only inches away from each other. Ricardo continued to shout. Felipe didn't say anything, but he had an evil look on his face.

"Stop it. Stop it!" said Flor. She pushed the men apart and stood between them. Ricardo moved, but he kept shouting. Flor said, *"Ricardo, shut up. Felipe, go inside."*

After one more mean glare at Ricardo, Felipe turned to go. All of them saw Betina, standing in the middle of the living room. "*Are you fighting?*" she asked.

"No, no," said Ricardo, immediately. *"I was just talking loudly. Telling your uncle some things. Come here, Betina."*

But Betina didn't come. *"Mama,"* she said.

Flor rushed to her. She picked her up and hugged her. "*Don't be frightened,*" she whispered. "*Daddy and Felipe were a little angry with each other. No one is mad at you.*"

She carried Betina to Ricardo. When he held out his arms, Betina went to him.

❖

My Journal, Monday, October 22

Today I am very angry because the father of my child no do come saturday. I *le dije* why? The *dijo* because *tengo* much work. I think he no do like my brother. The week last, my brother y the father fight.

Karen:

He didn't (did not) come at all? That is terrible. I understand why you are angry. Betina needs to see her father.

Flor read Karen's written response in her journal while Karen sat next to her.

Karen said, "*Le dije* in English is 'I told him.' But I think the idea you want to express is 'I asked him why.' Then 'He said because he has a lot of work. I don't think he likes my brother.' Remember last week when we talked about contractions? 'Don't' is the same as . . . what?"

Flor thought a minute. "Do not?"

"Yes. Good. Also, don't forget about the 's' on the end of the present third person singular. 'Likes.'"

"OK. Thank you, Karen."

The teacher moved on to the woman from Indonesia sitting on her right. Flor waved to Senem, who was sitting across the room. She turned to Carmen.

Carmen said, *"So Ricardo didn't come again? That's twice this month, isn't it?"*

"Yes. I'm very angry with him. Betina gets so excited when she thinks he's coming and is so disappointed when he doesn't. I stopped telling her when he is supposed to come. Now that I'm working Saturdays and saving a little money, I don't want to call in sick."

"You can leave Betina with us if you have to. Mario loves kids. The more the merrier. He doesn't see Betina during the week because he's always at work."

"Thanks, Carmen. I love coming to class where everyone is so nice. Ricardo and my brother don't like each other at all. They even fought in front of Betina last week. I don't want Betina to see and hear that. She doesn't understand, and it frightens her. I don't really understand either. They are both so certain they are right."

"Bull-headed. *Karen taught us that word last week, remember?*"

Flor laughed. "You hit the nail on the head!"

Halloween came on October 31st. Lena offered to make a costume for Betina. Flor was happy to have her do it. Lena had a sewing machine and was very creative. Work and English class took up so much of Flor's time, and she didn't want to spend her evenings sewing. Betina looked darling in the clown costume her grandmother made.

The pre-school class joined the rest of the school in the annual Halloween parade. The principal, dressed as a ghost, led the procession, starting with the oldest kids. As the line snaked through each classroom, the students got to see everyone's costumes before joining the parade at the end. When the whole school walked around the playground outside, people slowed down their cars and honked.

Some parents walked with the children and wore masks or funny hats. Flor wore the witch's hat she borrowed from Karen. She had a camera and took pictures of Betina with her big, red clown's nose and white face paint. Lena came to watch the parade and help with the class party afterward. She said to Flor, "*With all the cookies and punch, Betina won't want dinner. Are you taking her out to trick-or-treat later?"*

Flor answered, *"Oh, trick-or-treat! All I hear about is trick-or-treat! All Betina talks about is going door-to-door asking for candy. I'm taking time off from work so I can be here now, but Carmen said she can take Betina with them. It sounds fun. I wish I could go, too."*

Lena hesitated. *"Ricardo asked me to find out your plans. He wants to take Betina trick-or-treating."*

Flor looked at her mother-in-law. *"Why didn't he ask me himself?"*

"I don't know. I don't like being the messenger. He asked me this morning. I told him I would do it this time, but not again."

"What do you think, Lena? I want Betina to share special things with her father, but I don't want Ricardo to think he can have his way any time he wants."

"I understand," Lena said. *"But Halloween only comes once a year. Maybe I could take Betina home today, Ricardo could take her out trick-or-treating in our neighborhood, and then you could come get her after work or even tomorrow. Then you can work late and make up the time you are taking off this afternoon."*

"Alright. And this way, Ricardo doesn't have to see Felipe."

It was already dark by 5:00. The leaves turned red and yellow, then brown, and then fell to the ground. Sometimes it was windy, and the leaves swirled all over. On the weekends, Flor and Betina saw people outside dressed in sweaters and long pants. They were raking the leaves into big piles and filling large plastic bags with them.

One day late in the month, Carmen entered their classroom with a big smile on her face. Even before she sat down, she said to Flor excitedly, *"Guess what? There's an apartment for rent in my building. The manager told me this morning. He's going to paint it this weekend. It's only a studio, which means it has a kitchen, bathroom, and living room, but no bedroom. But the rent is cheap. It's $400 a month. I told him not to rent it until I talked to you, and he said he'll wait until tomorrow to put up a sign. Isn't that great?"*

"Yes! I can't believe it. But I don't have very much money saved."

"You can stop paying me for a while. I never told my husband about the money anyway. I opened a savings account at the bank across the street after Karen took us over there."

Flor was distracted from thinking about the apartment. *"You mean you went and filled in the application and talked to them by yourself?"*

"Yes. They were great. I had $100 to deposit.

They gave me a little book to record my deposits and said I would get a statement every month telling me what interest I am earning."

"I think I'll do that. It's better and safer than keeping cash at home in a box. But even if I don't pay you, I don't know if I have enough for the rent and a security deposit. And I want to pay you. It's important to me. You take good care of Betina."

Carmen said, *"Thanks. Rosy and I enjoy it. We can work something out. The manager said you have to pay the first and last months' rent. There's no lease. I think that's why the rent is so cheap."*

"Is it good to have a lease?"

"Sometimes. The lease can protect you if you and your landlord have a disagreement."

"I'll have to ask Ricardo to help me," said Flor. *"I know I don't have $800. I don't want to lose the chance to get the apartment. Do you think the manager will hold it for me? I can go talk to him tomorrow morning before work."*

Carmen said, *"I'll ask him. He's nice. He wants to have someone we know in the apartment, not a stranger."*

Flor thought a moment. *"I'll call Ricardo from work on my break."*

"OK. Then, in the morning, you and Betina can come over. I'll introduce you to the manager, and you can see the apartment."

The two women didn't have time to discuss it anymore. Karen was ready to start class.

Flor was making Whoppers at work when Linda called out, *"Flor! The phone is for you. It's an emergency!"*

Flor's heart stopped. Betina, she thought. Linda took over for her at the grill and she hurried to the phone.

"Yes?"

"This is Carmen. Flor, Betina is hurt. I'm so sorry. It's all my fault—"

Flor interrupted her. *"Carmen, I'm coming right now."*

"No, wait. We're at Denver Health. I came in the ambulance. Come to the emergency room."

"Emergency room? Oh, no. I'm coming. I'll be there as soon as I can."

Flor ran to David's office in the back of the restaurant.

"I have to go. My daughter is hurt. She's in the emergency room," she said.

"What happened?" asked David.

"I don't know! Carmen, her baby-sitter, just called. An accident, I think."

David stood up. *"How are you going to get there?"*

"I don't know."

"I'll take you," he said. *"Do you want to call anyone first?"*

"Oh! Yes, I should call Ricardo."

David went to tell Linda that he and Flor were leaving. Flor called Ricardo at work and told him what she knew. He said, *"I'll meet you at the hospital!"* and hung up. Even though she was worried, Flor noticed that Ricardo didn't ask how she was going to get there.

The hospital was close to the Burger King, and Flor and David arrived quickly. David parked in a 20-minute parking zone, and they both got out of the car and ran into the emergency room. Flor went to the first desk.

"My daughter!" she said. "My daughter is here?"

"What's her name?"

"Betina Pacheco."

"How do you spell the last name?"

David took over. "P-A-C-H-E-C-O. She's a little girl. She's been in some kind of accident."

"Yes, Room 3. Go right down that hall."

At that moment, Ricardo burst into the emergency room.

"Flor," he called. *"Where is she?"*

The woman at the desk looked at Flor and raised her eyebrows.

"He is papa," Flor said. "Father. He is father."

"Oh, Room 3," the woman repeated.

David touched Flor's shoulder. *"Flor, will you be OK? I have to go back to work."*

"Yes, thank you," said Flor.

"Call me, and let me know how Betina is. I hope she'll be alright."

"Thank you," said Flor again.

David left, and Flor and Ricardo hurried down the hall. *"I called my mother and Maria,"* said Ricardo. *"They'll be here as soon as possible."*

Flor nodded. She opened the door to Room 3. Carmen was sitting beside a hospital bed. Betina was in the bed, a bandage covered her shaved head. Her eyes were closed, and her little face looked pale. Fluid dripped through a tube into a vein in her arm.

Flor rushed over to the bed and took her daughter's hand. *"Betina-tina. Little One."*

"I am so sorry, Flor," said Carmen, starting to cry. *"It's my fault."*

"Calm down," said Ricardo. *"What happened?"*

"Who are you?" asked Carmen.

"I'm Ricardo. Who are you?"

"This is Carmen," said Flor. *"My friend. Betina's baby-sitter."* She turned her attention to Carmen. *"What happened?"*

"I was on the Internet. Rosy and Betina asked if they could play on the balcony in front of the apartment. I said yes. I told them to leave the door open and not to go near the stairs. Suddenly, I heard a loud noise, and Rosy started to scream. I ran outside. Oh, Flor, I shouldn't have let them go outside! I was distracted by the Internet."

"Did she fall off the balcony?" asked Ricardo.

"No, she fell down the concrete stairs. All the way, from the top to the bottom. She hurt her head. She was bleeding, a lot of blood. I screamed, and the manager came out. He called 911."

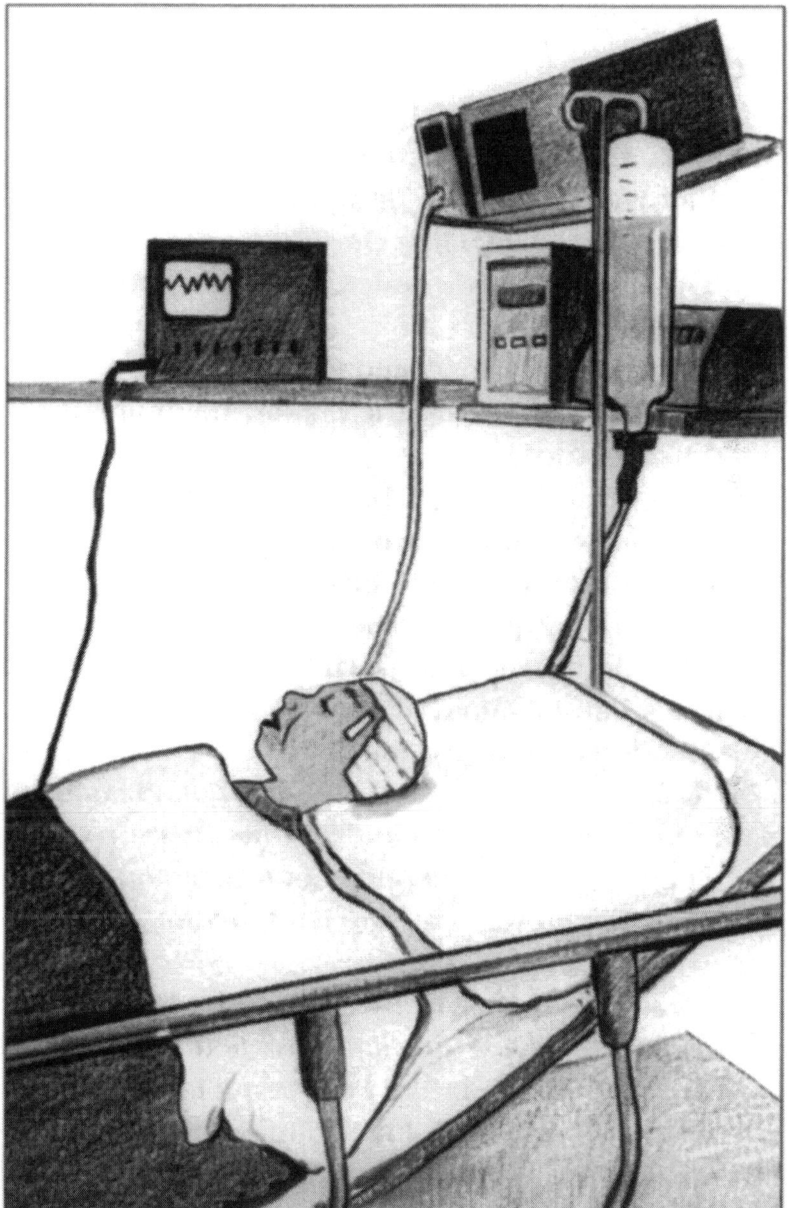

"Is anything broken?" asked Flor. *"Her arms, her legs?"*

"The doctor doesn't think so. But she never woke up, Flor. She's still unconscious from the fall."

Flor leaned over her daughter's face. *"Wake up, Little One. Wake up, Little One."*

The door opened, and a man in a white coat came in.

"Here's the doctor," said Carmen.

"Mr. Pacheco?" said the doctor, holding out his hand to Ricardo.

"Yes," said Ricardo. They shook hands.

The doctor and Ricardo spoke in English for a long time. Flor tried her best to understand, but they talked very quickly. They used too many words that she didn't recognize. Then the doctor shook Ricardo's hand again and left.

"What did he say?" asked Flor.

"She has a concussion. It's bad that she doesn't wake up, but her breathing and heart are regular. They're just watching her now, but they may have to do some tests to see why she isn't awake yet."

"What kind of tests?"

Ricardo sat down by the bed. *"The doctor described one where they'll put her in a big tube and take a picture of her brain. I've seen it on TV."*

Carmen turned to Flor, *"I'm going home. The apartment manager is taking care of Rosy right now. Mario will be home soon, and I'll come back."*

"OK," said Flor. She stroked Betina's hand. Carmen hugged Flor, nodded to Ricardo, and left.

Flor and Ricardo sat in silence and watched their beautiful daughter breathe. Finally, Ricardo said, *"Why did you pick someone like Carmen to take care of Betina? This never would have happened at my mother's house."*

Rage filled Flor. *"It was an accident! It could have happened to anyone!"*

"It was an accident, but Carmen isn't careful. She let the girls go outside without supervision. Betina will go back to my mother's house when she wakes up."

"Why are we talking about this now?" Flor carefully placed Betina's hand back on the bed. *"We should be talking about Betina. What if she needs extra care? What if she never wakes up? Who's going to pay for all of this? I can't pay!"* Flor was so mad she was shaking. *"And anyway, the best person to take care of Betina is me. But you made sure she can't have me. This is not my fault, or even Carmen's fault. This is your fault."*

"My fault? Just like a woman to make everything the man's fault! But I take care of my child. I buy her clothes. And I pay for her health insurance. Insurance will cover her hospital bills and tests. She's hurt and lying in bed, and all you can think of is money." Ricardo spoke in a harsh, low whisper.

"Why didn't you tell me about the insurance? I'm

her mother! I should know if she has insurance. That's just like you, always sneaking around, hiding things. I can't stand that."

Ricardo snapped, "*You don't have to stand it. I'm not with you anymore.*"

Flor glared at Ricardo over the bed. He glared back.

From the bed, Betina stirred. She coughed and opened her eyes. "*Mama? Papa?*"

CHAPTER 8

Betina had to stay in the hospital overnight for observation. Maria, Lena, and Carmen all sat with Ricardo and Flor until midnight, and then everyone went home except for the two of them. After their fight, Flor thought they would never speak again, but as the hours passed, they began to talk to each other.

"Carmen is good to Betina," said Flor. *"You saw how worried she was. And she's my friend. I don't have very many friends."*

Ricardo nodded. *"I know. I kept you all to myself when we were married."*

"We're still married," said Flor. *"We never got divorced."*

"Oh, that common law thing. We don't fit. I asked a lawyer," said Ricardo. *"There are four requirements. One is that you have to intend to be married. We never even talked about it."*

"Yes, we did," said Flor.

"Do you want to fight again?" asked Ricardo.

Flor didn't want to fight. *"No."*

"I don't want your life to be hard," said Ricardo. *"Flor, I still love you and Betina. I want to help you."*

Flor's eyes filled with tears. *"If you love us, why did you leave us?"*

"I don't know. You were gone a long time. I love Sandra, too. She was here with me."

"Her name is Sandra?" asked Flor.

Ricardo nodded.

Flor wiped her eyes. *"If you want to help Betina and me, help us get out of Felipe's house. I found a nice apartment, and I need help with the rent."*

"OK," said Ricardo.

"Don't you want to know how much it is?"

"I'll pay whatever it is. I want Betina and you to have a home."

"Lucky for you it's only $400 a month."

They both smiled. They were exhausted, but Betina was going to be fine.

❖

Flor and Betina moved into the apartment the first weekend in December. Felipe helped her take over all their clothes and the few household items they had. In the mid-afternoon, Ricardo came to pick up Betina for her first overnight stay at his house. He surprised Flor with the double bed from their old apartment.

"We have another one," he said.

Carmen and her husband offered to take Flor to the flea market to look for other furniture. They found a dining room table with four chairs that only had a few scratches, and a comfortable but ugly sofa.

"This is enough to start with," said Flor. *"Besides, I don't have anymore money."* She gave a little smile. She felt satisfied.

❖

My Journal, Monday, December 17

I love my apartment. Is small and soft. We look the beautiful snow. The grandmother of Betina give she the rope the Christmas lights. Betina, she head is better now. I excite the Secret Santa. My manager the Burger King is my friend. He have the party. I go the party. The Christmas trees is pretty. I miss *Las Posadas*.

Karen:

Flor, your apartment sounds *cozy* (not soft). The snow is beautiful. Do you *look at it* or *see it* or *watch it fall* from your apartment window? That was nice of Betina's grandmother to give her a *string* of Christmas lights. Are they all white or many colors? I *am excited about* our Secret Santa gift exchange, too. It is nice that your manager *at* Burger King is your friend. Did you already go *to* the party, or will you go this weekend? Christmas trees *are* pretty. Will you tell the class about *Las Posadas*? I think everyone will be interested to learn about this Mexican custom. If I forget to tell you personally, have a very Merry Christmas. I'll see you in the new year.

❖

My Journal, Wednesday, February 20

Senem came my home the Sunday. She maked special food her country with rice. I maked *posole*. Her son and my daughter played. Senem has hope her sister coming. She is sad her family do not live here. I think I have luck for Carmen live next door me and for me no am pregnant.

Karen:

Senem and you made some good food. Why didn't you bring some to me? You are lucky to have a friend next door. Senem misses her family. Let's have a baby shower for her. Do you know what that is? We'll have a party in class, and everyone will give her a present for the new baby. We'll "shower" her with presents.

Flor thought the idea of a baby shower was wonderful.

"I want to help," she told Karen.

"Great," said Karen. "But we won't have the baby shower until her sister is here."

After class Senem called Flor's name. Flor waited for her. Senem handed her a package.

"Thank you for having me in your home," she said.

Flor opened the package. A beautiful blue scarf the looked like the sky was inside. She unfolded it and draped it over her head. It felt soft and smelled good, like Senem.

"It's from Turkey," said Senem. "Now you are good Turkish woman!"

Flor laughed. "Yes! Thank you. Is beautiful."

Betina pulled the scarf off of Flor's head. "Mama, I want to wear it. To cover my head!"

"You don't need it anymore," said Flor. "Your hair is growing back. I'll let you wear it later."

Senem said, "She wants a scarf, yes?"

"This one!" said Flor.

"I'll bring her one," said Senem, smiling.

"Good!" said Betina.

"Betina, did you understand what Senem said?" asked Flor.

"Of course, Mama," said Betina. *"I understand everybody."*

Flor raised her eyebrows, and then laughed. She said to Senem, "She speak English. She learn."

"Children learn fast," said Senem. "Hasan and Betina spoke English at your home. Did you hear them?"

"No," said Flor. "I was learn cook your food. I was busy."

Flor, Senem, and Carmen walked out of the building together, and then Flor hurried to work.

When she arrived Linda was there. Flor was surprised to see her. Usually David was there at the beginning of the shift, and then Linda came later.

"Flor, David and I want to talk to you," said Linda.

Flor wondered what was wrong. *"Is everything OK?"* she asked.

"Oh, yes. Don't worry."

Linda and Flor walked to the back of the restaurant to David's small office. He was sitting behind his desk.

"Please, sit down," he said, smiling. *"Linda and I have good news for you."*

Flor sat down. She felt nervous. "What is it?"

"We want to offer you a promotion. One of our cashiers quit. Your English has improved so much that we want you to be the cashier."

Flor shook her head in disbelief. *"I don't know enough English yet."*

David and Linda laughed. *"You know more than you think,"* said Linda. *"Say yes! I can train you tonight. I think you'll make a wonderful cashier."*

"I don't know. . . ." said Flor, her voice full of

doubt. What if David and Linda were wrong? What if the very first customer confused Flor so much that David and Linda were disappointed in her?

"Sometimes English sounds like Chinese to me," she said. *"Other times I understand what the person is saying, but I can't answer."*

"I heard you talking to a customer just the other day," said Linda. *"You did fine. Besides, I'll teach you most of the things you'll have to say."*

"Flor, you're one of our best workers," said David. *"You are responsible, you get here on time, and you always agree to work extra hours. And, we pay cashiers more. It's a position of trust and responsibility, so you'll get a dollar more per hour."*

Flor was working 48 hours a week, including the overtime on Saturday. *"That's $48 extra,"* she thought. *"I can get a telephone."*

"OK," she said, *"Thank you. I'll do it."*

"Great," said David. He reached across the desk and shook her hand.

"Let's get to work," said Linda.

Flor worked hard that night, learning how to run the cash register, make correct change, and take orders. She learned "Would you like a drink with that?" and many other phrases. She made a lot of mistakes, but Linda helped her correct them.

"Everyone makes mistakes at first," said Linda. *"Now you'll know what to do when I'm not here. And, you'll make fewer mistakes as you get used to the job."*

"I don't want to think about what I'll do when you're not here," said Flor.

Linda laughed. *"Don't worry. I'll work with you at least two more times."*

Most of the customers were polite and patient and spoke clearly. Some were in a hurry and seemed impatient, and some spoke loudly.

"They seem to think loud speech will help me understand," Flor told Linda.

One man got angry because she forgot to specify "no tomatoes" on his hamburger.

"I'm allergic to tomatoes," he said. "Can't you people get anything right?"

Flor became confused and forgot every English word she knew.

"I'm so sorry, sir," said Linda. "We're training a new cashier. We'll make you a fresh hamburger, and here's a coupon for a free drink." When he left, she showed Flor where the coupons were. *"Saying you're sorry usually helps a lot, but when the customer is in a bad mood, a coupon for something free makes him feel much better. Just stay calm and polite because if you get angry that makes them madder."*

By the end of the evening Flor's head ached and her feet hurt. She sat down with Linda for a soda pop before she went home.

"Well, do you think you'll like it?" asked Linda, in Spanish.

"People talk so fast," said Flor. *"But I under-*

stood almost everything they said. It's challenging, but yes, I think I'll like it."

"It will get easier and easier."

"Do you promise?"

"I promise," laughed Linda.

When Flor got home, she told Carmen about the promotion and the raise. Her friend hugged her.

"You deserve it," she said. *"You work so hard. Ricardo must realize what a fool he is to leave a woman like you."*

Flor shrugged. *"I try not to think about that,"* she said.

Ever since the accident, Ricardo called Flor every day to find out how Betina was doing. She was fine, but he kept calling. Flor enjoyed speaking with him and telling him what Betina did and said. Sometimes he made her sad and mad by talking about his new family, but often he made her laugh at his jokes.

One Saturday he arrived early at Flor's apartment to pick up Betina. Flor was happy to see him, but Betina wasn't.

"Oh, no," she said. *"I can't go yet. My doll is at Rosy's house. Rosy is braiding her hair. We have to wait."*

Ricardo sat down at the kitchen table. *"I'll wait long enough to drink one cup of coffee."*

"Oh, do you think I'm going to make you coffee?" teased Flor. *"You must think I'm your wife or something."*

Ricardo looked surprised. Flor was surprised, too. Why did she say that? Then, they both laughed.

"Betina, go see if Rosy is done while Papa drinks his coffee," said Flor, with a smile.

She made strong, instant coffee for both of them. They sat at the table and talked while Betina was gone. Ricardo told Flor about his job. He was making more money. His boss told him that he was his best worker. He just wanted him to learn to write better.

"Maybe you can find an English class like mine," said Flor. *"In fact, they have evening classes at the school. Maybe you can go to them. I learn something new every day."*

"I was thinking of the community college. Anyway, are you sure you're learning English in class and not from your friend?"

"What friend?"

"You know, the guy who brought you to the hospital when Betina was hurt."

"Oh, yes, a little. But we speak a lot of Spanish. He likes to practice."

Ricardo winked. *"What else does he like to practice with you?"*

Flor laughed in disbelief. *"Are you serious? He's my boss! David is a good boss, and a good friend, but he's married. It makes a difference to me, you know."* She picked up their cups from the table and took them to the sink. *"That's funny, me and David."*

When she turned around, she found Ricardo right there, standing in front of her.

"It's not so funny," he said, softly. *"You're so pretty. I'm sure your boss sees how pretty you are."*

Flor blushed. Ricardo put his arms around her and pulled her to him. Even after all these months, it felt so familiar to be in his embrace. It felt good.

She leaned her head against his chest and inhaled. How easy it would be to stay this way, with his strong arms around her.

"Flor," he whispered, *"I want you back in my life. We were happy. We have a child. We should be together."*

Flor felt like she was dreaming. This was not real. She spent so many nights hugging Betina close to her and wishing Ricardo was there. Now, he was saying all the things she thought she wanted to hear.

"Think of it. You, me, and Betina here together in this nice little apartment. We'll get a new sofa that pulls out and makes a bed for Betina."

Flor thought her heart was going to burst, it was beating so hard.

"I'll come every Saturday morning, early, and spend all day and all night. Betina and I will leave on Sunday, and Sandra will never know. I'll say it's a new part of my job to be gone on Saturdays," Ricardo whispered.

Flor caught her breath and pulled away from Ricardo.

"What?"

"Don't worry. I have it all planned," said Ricardo. He tried to embrace her again.

Flor pushed Ricardo away. Did she struggle for months, spend all those lonely nights, worry about money and Betina, just to become Ricardo's mistress? Was he crazy? What about Sandra? How could Flor treat her so badly? What lies was Ricardo telling her?

"You like me now, but what about when I came back from Mexico and had nothing? You can't be serious about this." In English she said, "You want to have your cake and eat it, too."

"What does that mean?" asked Ricardo, looking embarrassed because he didn't know.

"I learned it in my English class. Ask your boss what it means."

Ricardo sat down at the table again. *"Flor, you seem mad. Why are you mad? I thought we were friends again."*

"That is what we are. Friends, nothing more. Ricardo, you left me. You made a decision to marry someone new. You call your new wife and her children your family. I accept that. I miss you, but I don't want to be the second woman in your life. Do you understand why?"

"No, not really. You work all the time anyway. I can be here when you aren't working."

"I work all the time because I have to support Betina and me!"

Ricardo sighed. *"OK. I can give you a little more money."*

"No! I don't want to be paid to be your mistress. The answer is no."

Ricardo didn't look angry, but he did look disappointed. All those months, thought Flor, he was just waiting for this moment so he could have two wives. She looked closely at her ex-husband. He was handsome, yes. He was funny, and he loved his daughter. He was also unreliable and a liar, and Flor didn't want a man like that living with her, even for one day.

"Things are fine the way they are right now," she said.

Betina came running into the apartment.

"Look at my doll," she said. *"She's beautiful."*

The doll had tight little braids sticking out all over her head. She looked terrible.

"Yes, she is," said Flor.

"Almost as beautiful as my girl," said Ricardo, picking Betina up.

Flor handed Ricardo Betina's suitcase. She kissed Betina and then kissed Ricardo on the cheek.

"You're my friend now. My good friend," she said.

She thought Ricardo was going to say something mean, but suddenly he smiled. He winked at her again.

"You can always change your mind. I'll see you next Saturday."

Flor shook her head in disbelief as she closed the door behind Betina and Ricardo. That man was full of surprises. Flor was surprised at herself, too. She said no to Ricardo. He offered her more money and his love, and she said no. Now, it was her choice, not Ricardo's, to be alone with Betina. After a few minutes, she smiled. She was in control of her own life.

Later, at work, she thought about Ricardo again. Why wasn't she angry with him? It was an insult to offer to be with her one day a week, wasn't it? Maybe I don't love him anymore, she thought.

"Excuse me, Earth to Flor," said David, walking over to her. "Are you going to give these people their food?"

"Oh! I'm sorry," she said to the young man and woman who were waiting. "Two Number Four Combos. Have a nice day."

On her break she sat with David and Linda and ate her lunch.

"What are you thinking about?" said David. *"You weren't paying as much attention as you usually do."*

"A strange thing happened to me this morning," Flor explained. She told them about Ricardo and his offer, but not about his suspicions about David.

David listened and nodded, but he didn't say

anything. Linda said, *"I would have slapped his cheek, not kissed it."*

"That's why you're not married," said David.

"But neither am I!" said Flor. For the first time, she really felt this was true.

CHAPTER 9

My Journal, Monday, May 6

On Sunday I and Betina went Fort Collins with my brother. It was one special day. Betina's father did not take her for Saturday night so she can come with me. We went Fort Collins to see my cousins. We ate good food and we walked outside in the beautiful sunshine. We talked very much. I told my cousins about my life. They are sad Ricardo left Betina and me, but I said them I am happy now. My life is hard, but also my life is more good.

Karen:

It is embarrassing to tell family and friends when something happens like your husband leaving. Was this the first time you told your cousins about Ricardo leaving you? I know this has been a very hard year for you, but I am proud of how you have persevered (kept working). Things will get better and better! You have only missed a few English classes even though you work so hard at Burger King. Now, we only have three weeks of school left before the summer break. I hope you will come back to class next fall!

❖

Flor was amazed at how quickly the school year had passed. She started English classes in September, and now it was already May. She had learned a lot of English, but she had much more to learn. She could talk to her friend, Senem, and she was doing well at her cashier job, but she still was confused at the supermarket or when she talked on the telephone.

One day in class she said, "Karen, I have question for interest everybody."

"Great. What is it?"

"When you speak, I understand all. But sometime when other person, American person, speak, I no understand anything."

"You don't understand anything?"

"I understand a little. Half."

Karen nodded. "Well, half is better than before. When you started classes, you understood almost nothing."

"When I . . . . when will I understand all?" asked Flor.

"You think Karen is magic, she know everything?" said Carmen.

The whole class began to laugh, and Karen and Flor laughed, too. When the laughter stopped, Senem spoke.

"This is my second year of English class," she said, slowly. "Sometime, I am very tired. I don't want to come. But I remember my first months in America. I went to my son's school, and everyone talked to me. I just smiled and smiled. My husband answered for me. I felt like puppet. You know, toy with strings being pulled by some person to make it move? Now, I understand almost everything people say. If I don't understand, I guess."

Flor nodded. "Two years." That didn't seem like such a long time.

"For Senem, two years," said Karen. "But she speaks English almost all the time. People in America don't speak Turkish. I read that it can take up to seven years of continuous study and speaking to become really fluent in a language."

"Too long!" said Carmen, making the whole class laugh again.

"It depends on you," said Karen. "Everyone is different. But Flor, you are doing very well."

"Yes, yes," said Carmen. "Flor is the teacher favorite."

"You're all my favorites!" said Karen.

The class continued, but Flor still wondered when she would be able to understand everything that was said to her. It helped to know that Senem, who spoke very good English, still guessed sometimes.

"For me, two years," she decided. *"Carmen is right. Seven years is too long!"*

At work that night, she said to David and Linda, "No more Spanish during work. Only during break. You have to help me with my English."

"But I love speaking Spanish," said David.

"Me, too," said Flor. "But I need more practice. Please help me!"

Linda and David both agreed that they would try to remember. Flor thanked them and got to work. She had been a cashier for more than three months. She was very comfortable taking orders, but she rarely greeted the customers. Linda always said, "Hello, how can I help you?" or "Can I take your order?" or even, "What'll you have today?" Flor usually smiled with a questioning look on her face and waited for the customer to speak first.

Also, every day at least one customer wanted to chat, and then she had problems. She just smiled more and said, "I speak only a little English." She decided that was going to change. She would be more like Carmen, bold and talkative. When the first customer of her shift came in, she called out, "How may I help you today, sir?" in a loud, firm voice.

The customer looked surprised and said, "Well, I don't know yet."

"I am here to help," she said, cheerfully.

The customer looked behind him. He was the only one in line. "OK," he said. He continued to look at the menu.

"Today is a nice sunny day," said Flor, when he finally seemed to make up his mind.

"Yeah. Number 6."

Flor rang up his order. "It's a little cold," she said.

"Whatever," said the customer. He handed her some money.

"But with sun the cold is no too bad," she said.

"Look, I didn't ask for a weather report. I just want my food," said the customer.

"Sorry," said Flor. "Coming right away." She grimaced and thought, next time I'll wait for the customer to begin the conversation.

The days passed quickly. Flor worked, went to school, practiced her English, and took care of Betina. She didn't have time to do very much more, but one Sunday she got up early and looked in her closet. All her clothes looked tired and gray. She didn't want to wear any of them.

"Betina and I are going shopping," she decided. She took the bus to Lena's house. She arrived at the same time as Ricardo and Betina.

"You just wanted to see me twice in one weekend, didn't you?" Ricardo joked. He hugged and kissed Betina and left.

Betina and Flor went in the house to say hello

to Lena. She was sitting at the kitchen table drinking a cup of coffee. Maria was there, too. Flor hadn't seen her since Betina was in the hospital.

"Hello, Betina. Hello, Flor," said Maria. She sounded cheerful and friendly.

"Good morning," said Flor. She kissed Lena on the cheek, and Betina climbed up into Maria's lap.

"What are you doing today, Aunt Maria?" she asked.

"Nothing. I don't have anything to do."

Betina frowned. *"Well, you can come with Mama and me,"* she said.

"Where are you going?" asked Maria.

"I don't know," said Betina. *"Where are we going, Mama?"*

"Well, we're going shopping. I think we need some new clothes," said Flor.

"Oooh! Aunt Maria, we're going shopping! You can come with us."

"That would be very nice," said Maria. *"Can I come, Flor? We can go in my car."*

Flor was surprised. Maria was being very friendly to offer a ride. She had not offered any help at all since September. Even when Betina was hurt and Flor needed extra baby-sitting help, Maria had not helped.

"Sure," said Flor. *"We won't say no to a ride in a car, will we Betina?"*

"Goody!" said Betina. She gave Maria a hug.

They decided to go to the big discount chain

store, because they had the best prices on clothing. *"They have a good selection, too,"* said Maria. *"Maybe Betina will let me buy her a little present."*

Betina loved the store. She tried on many dresses, pants, and shoes. Finally, they found a pair of cute white sandals that fit. She selected a sleeveless flowered dress, but she couldn't decide between a pair of jeans and a t-shirt with colorful stitching.

Flor said, *"Let's get both. You're growing so fast. All your clothes are too small."*

"OK," said Betina. *"Now, I need a hat."*

Maria and Flor laughed. Maria linked her arm with Flor's.

"She's just like a little adult, isn't she?" she said.

"She has a mind of her own," said Flor.

"Just like her mother."

The two women smiled at each other.

"And just like her aunt!" said Flor.

They shopped all morning. Flor bought herself a colorful blouse, some red sandals, and a bottle of nail polish.

"I can't let my toes go naked," she said.

"Will you paint mine, too?" asked Betina. *"I don't want naked toes, either."*

"Of course," said Flor.

Maria bought Betina a hat to go with her dress and, in return, Flor bought Maria a tablecloth she admired. *"This is perfect for the next time you and*

Betina come to my house for dinner," said Maria. *"Thank you."*

Surprise after surprise. This must be her way of apologizing, thought Flor, but she said, *"That would be fun."*

They all had lunch at the hot dog stand, and finally, they got in Maria's car to go home.

"Shopping is fun," said Betina. *"I like shopping with you, Aunt Maria. You can come with us every time."*

"OK!" said Maria.

She dropped them off at their apartment and waved as she left. Carmen was sitting outside in the sunshine.

"Was that Maria?" she asked.

"Yes," said Flor.

"When did she become your friend again?"

"Today," said Flor.

Carmen stood up. *"That's nice, isn't it?"*

"Yes, it is. She's Betina's aunt, and I want to be friends with her."

Flor and Betina walked up the steps. Rosy came out of her apartment.

"Mama, they're back!" she said. *"Let's go to the park!"*

"We were waiting for Betina," said Carmen. *"It's such a nice day; we want to go to the park. Maybe Senem and Hasan will be there. Can Betina come with us?"*

"Please, Mama, say yes," said Betina.

Flor needed to do laundry and go grocery shopping, but she decided that she needed a little more fun, too. *"We'll both come,"* she said.

The little girls cheered. They all walked slowly to the park. They enjoyed the sunshine and the flowers and noticed many other people out walking, running, and riding bicycles. Betina and Rosy walked in front of Flor and Carmen. They held hands and giggled.

"Look at those two girls," said Carmen. *"They're getting so big. In September Rosy will be in preschool."*

"They grow up so quickly. Betina will be in kindergarten!"

"I'll be so happy when Rosy is in school," said Carmen. *"I'm going to get a job. I'm going to work in a store. I want to sell clothes or shoes."*

"Really? You'll have to talk all the time!" said Flor.

"Yes. I want to talk all the time. And I want to be busy. I'm bored just staying home and taking care of Rosy."

"You are?"

"Sure!" said Carmen. *"I want to get out and work and make some money and be with other adults. You know what? I went to the Parent Teacher Student Association meeting last Wednesday."*

Carmen always amazed Flor. She was so bold, so brave.

"What did they talk about?" she asked.

"Oh, many things. The end-of-year picnic and a special meeting to organize the group for next year. I understood almost everything. Karen was there, too."

"She was?"

"Yes. She asked me if I want to help her start a Spanish-language PTSA. I said yes. Do you want to help us?"

"I don't know," said Flor. *"I don't have very much free time."*

"Think about it," said Carmen. *"You and I will go to the English language meetings. The next day, we'll have a meeting for Spanish-speaking parents. If they have any ideas, they can tell us and we can tell the PTSA. It will be fun!"*

Flor thought about it all afternoon. Later, as they started to go back home from the park, she said, *"Yes, I'll help you."*

"Great," said Carmen. *"We'll talk to Karen about it tomorrow."*

Carmen and Rosy went home, and Flor and Betina went to the grocery store. They bought chicken and rice for dinner and went home and cooked it. Betina set the table with plates and forks and poured water into glasses. They talked as they ate, and then Flor put Betina to bed.

After Betina was asleep, Flor took the laundry down to the apartment building washing machine. While she waited she sat on a chair outside on the balcony. It was still warm. She felt good.

She thought about the lovely summer evenings to come, when it would stay light until 9:00. Maybe she and Maria would go dancing like they used to when Flor and Ricardo were married. Maria had danced with lots of men, and now so could Flor. She thought about Ricardo. She liked him, but she didn't love him. She didn't need him anymore.

CHAPTER 10

My Journal, Monday, May 13

I am excite. I am go to party at the house of my manager for the work. He invited me to come yesterday. It is one barbecue and I will take something of food. Betina is invite and other childs will be in the party. I am happy for my very nice manager.

Karen:

The barbecue sounds like fun. Will you take Mexican food? The mistakes you are making now are minor compared to a few months ago. I can tell you use your dictionary because you don't use any Spanish words. I underlined some of the grammar mistakes. Can you figure out the correct forms? If not, ask another student. I'll check your journal next time to see how you did.

The day of the party seemed to come sooner than Flor expected. She was nervous. She had so much to do to get ready, and she still didn't know what to wear.

"Have you ever been to an American party, Carmen?" Flor asked her friend. They were in Flor's apartment making *mole* for the barbecue at David's house.

Carmen stuck her finger in the stew, which was rich with spices and chocolate. *"Mmm. This is so good. I went to some parties at American people's houses before Mario and I got married, but they were adult parties. We stood around and shouted at each other because the music was so loud. I don't think this barbecue will be the same at all. For one thing, it's in the daytime and outside, and both kids and adults will be there."*

"I'm scared. I hope they like this mole. Do you think it's too hot?"

"No. I like spicy food, so I would add some more chili powder. But leave it like this for the party, to be on the safe side."

Flor felt relieved. *"I want people to like my food."*

"Americans love Mexican food. I do, too. Some Argentinian food is similar, but we eat a lot more meat than Mexican people eat."

"Can you see the girls? Are they OK?" Betina's accident was too recent for Flor to forget about checking on her often.

Carmen looked around the corner. *"They're fine. They're playing with their dolls."*

"Betina is going to wear her new jeans and t-shirt that we bought. It's so cute on her. But I'm not sure what I should wear. Do you think I should wear a dress?"

"Oh, no! Barbecues are informal. Don't you remember talking about that in class? Everyone will be wearing pants or shorts."

"Maybe I'll wear my new blouse with my navy blue pants. What do you think?"

Carmen laughed. *"I'd wear shorts, the shorter the better. But that sounds just right for you."*

The sun was still high in the sky when Flor and Betina arrived at David's house. They saw people in the yard and smelled hamburgers cooking. They went to the front door and rang the doorbell.

A woman came to the door. She was smiling. Her short blond hair and red shorts and top looked so American. Flor guessed that this was David's wife. She took a deep breath and said, "Hi. I am Flor. Is David at home?"

"Yes, of course. He's in the backyard. I'm Sarah, his wife. Come in. I've heard a lot about you. David is very glad you work for him. Is this your daughter?"

"I'm sorry. Yes, is Betina. I make *mole* for you. Here."

"Oh, how wonderful. Thank you. You didn't

have to bring anything. It smells delicious. I bet it won't last long." Sarah opened the screen door for Flor and Betina and led them through the house to the patio outside. Sarah and David's house was so nice, and so big. Sure, they had a little baby and a two-year-old, but Flor's whole apartment could fit in their living room.

Sarah put the *mole* on a long picnic table covered with a red-and-white checked tablecloth. No one was eating yet. Flor looked around. She saw David at the grill barbecuing hamburgers. Several adults were standing around talking with him. He saw her and waved for her to come over.

She and Betina headed that way. Betina was looking around. She saw four or five children playing on a swing set in one corner of the yard. Two boys were chasing each other near the house.

"Mama, can I go over there and play on the swing?"

"Yes. Have fun but be careful."

"I will."

Flor watched her daughter run over to the group and ask in English if she could play with them. She wished she felt as confident as Betina did.

David waved at her again, and Flor joined him at the grill. She didn't know any of the people talking to David. He introduced her to them and then pointed out other people in small groups on the patio and over by the garden. They were his neigh-

bors and his friends from college and their son's playgroup. She didn't see any of her co-workers except for Linda, who was just coming out of the house.

"Where are the other people from work? I see only Linda," Flor asked David.

"Oh, this isn't a work party. We only invited our family and friends," David answered with a smile.

Flor smiled back. She didn't know what to say. Finally, she stammered, "Th-thank you."

"Don't be embarrassed, Flor. It is great for us that you work at Burger King. I tell my wife about you all the time. She really wanted to meet you. She is very impressed by your progress in English and how you have learned the fast-food restaurant business so quickly. But now I need to turn the burgers. Are you hungry yet?"

Flor shook her head no. "I will go to see Linda," she said.

On her way, she stopped at the swing set to check on Betina. Her daughter was chatting away with two new friends. Flor was so proud of her, and a little in awe. *"It is so easy for her,"* thought Flor, *"and such a struggle for me. David gave me such a nice compliment. Now I need to live up to it. What would Carmen do? I want to be as brave as Betina and Carmen are."*

She headed toward the patio where Linda was having a lively discussion with some other people, and stood a few feet away listening to them. Linda turned to her.

"Come join us. We're talking about bilingual education," Linda told her in Spanish. *"Some of my friends speak Spanish."*

"Is OK," said Flor. "I speak English!"